BIG MACHINES

Fire Engines

David and Penny Glover

W
FRANKLIN WATTS
LONDON • SYDNEY

First published in 2004 by Franklin Watts
96 Leonard Street, London EC2A 4XD

Franklin Watts Australia
45-51 Huntley Street, Alexandria, NSW 2015

© Franklin Watts 2004

Series editor: Sarah Peutrill
Designer: Richard Langford
Art director: Jonathan Hair
Illustrator: Ian Thompson
Reading consultant: Margaret Perkins, Institute of Education, University of Reading
Picture credits: Dick Blume/Image Works/Topham: 15t. China Photo/Reuters/Corbis: 20b.
Photo supplied by E-ONE (Ocala, Florida): 23b. Firepix/Topham: 6, 11b, 13b, 14t, 15b, 16.
Hulton-Deutsch Collection/Corbis: 12. Photo courtesy of Mack Trucks Inc: 22c, 22b. Photo
courtesy of Oshkosh Truck Corporation: 23t. PA/Topham: 21t. Mark Reinstein/Image
Works/Topham: 7b. Reuters/Corbis: 21b. www.shoutpictures.com: front cover, 10, 11t, 18l, 18r.
Watts Publishing: Chris Fairclough 4, 8t, 9b, 13t, 17t, 17b, 19t, 19b /Chris Honeywell 7t, 9t, 14b.
Gloria Wright/Image Works/Topham: 8b. Every attempt has been made to clear copyright.
Should there be any inadvertent omission, please apply to the publisher for rectification.

With particular thanks to E-ONE (Ocala, Florida), Mack Trucks, Inc and Oshkosh Truck
Corporation for permission to use their photographs.

A CIP catalogue record for this book is available from the British Library.

ISBN 0 7496 5564 X

Printed in Malaysia

Contents

To the rescue

Fire engines are big rescue machines. They carry firefighters to all kinds of emergencies.

A fire engine pumps water through its hoses to fight a fire. Its long ladder rescues people trapped in a blazing building.

BIG FACT

A big fire engine is about 12 metres long and 2.5 metres wide.

At a road accident firefighters cut people from crashed cars. The fire engine carries all the tools they need.

Fire engines are painted in bright colours. This is so that they can be seen easily when they are racing to an emergency.

Ready and waiting!

The fire crew wait at the fire station for an emergency call.

The crew keep their fire engine in perfect condition, ready to go at a moment's notice.

The fire engine is filled with diesel fuel. ▶

◀ The crew clean the fire engine.

When an emergency call comes, the crew go into action. They slide down a pole into the garage.

▲ Using the pole is much quicker than walking down stairs.

The crew climb aboard, the garage doors open, and the fire engine is on its way.

In the cab

The driver's cab has the same controls as other big road trucks.

Mobile telephone

Steering wheel

Control panel

Radio

Fax machine

The cab also has satellite navigation. This shows the fastest route to the emergency.

In most fire engines there are seats behind the driver. These are for the rest of the fire crew.

Some of the crew's equipment is kept next to their seats.

At the emergency it is important to keep in touch with the control room.

◀ A firefighter speaks to the control room using the cab's radio.

Sirens and lights

In the past a fire engine had a bell to warn that it was coming. The firefighters held on to the sides as the engine raced along.

Bell

A bell is not loud enough for today's busy roads. A modern fire engine has a loud warning siren.

Siren

Light

The siren on this fire engine is between the warning lights.

A bright flashing light shows that the fire engine is near. People hear the siren, look for the light, and get out of the way.

At a fire, flashing lights warn people to keep away.

Fire hoses

At the fire, the firefighters reel out hoses to spray water onto the flames.

A hose is a hollow tube. A powerful pump pushes water out of the hose's nozzle.

nozzle

hose

The fire engine carries some water in a tank, but to fight a big blaze it must pump water from a fire hydrant, a river or a pond.

A firefighter unlocks a hydrant before attaching the hose.

fire hydrant

A monitor is a powerful water cannon. It can be pointed by hand, or operated by remote control.

A monitor ▶ pumps water from the top of a ladder onto a blazing house.

BIG FACT

A monitor pumps out enough water to fill a bath in a second!

A monitor is operated by the crew on top of a fire engine. ▶

Ladders and booms

Ladders help firefighters to fight fires in tall buildings.

The ladder operator uses the controls to raise the ladder and swing it into place.

The ladder on this fire engine is telescopic. Its sections slide over each other to make it longer.

This fire engine has a hydraulic boom. The boom unfolds to lift the platform high into the air.

Boom

Platform

Controls

A firefighter operates the boom from the bottom. ▶

A firefighter on the platform can make a rescue, or spray water into a burning building.

17

Rescue gear

The fire engine's lockers are filled with all kinds of rescue gear. There is something for every kind of emergency.

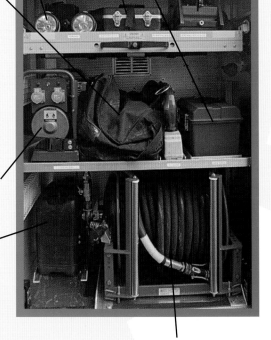

Chemical protection suits

Warning lights

Tool kits

Hydrant equipment

Spill bag (to soak up chemicals)

Portable pump

Lighting generator

Dry foam fire extinguishers

Black chocks (to put under cars to stop them from moving)

Hose

It is important to make sure all the equipment is in good working order.

A firefighter tests the breathing apparatus. ▶

Two firefighters clean their chemical protection suits in a special shower.

Fire boats and planes

When a ship catches fire a fire boat comes to the rescue. It pumps water from the sea to put out the flames.

Forest fires are the biggest fires of all. Planes and helicopters are needed to fight these huge blazes.

A fire helicopter flies over burning trees, and drops a load of water from a bag onto the flames below.

A fire plane releases water from a tank. It can carry more than 5,000 litres at a time.

Giant fire engines

The Super Pumper and Super Pumper Tender were the most powerful fire engines ever built. They fought fires in New York City, USA, from 1965 to 1982.

▲ The Super Pumper was used for very large fires.

◄ The water cannon on top of the Tender was very powerful. It could knock down thick walls.

The Striker 4500 is one of the most powerful fire engines in the world today. It puts out fires at airports.

▲ Even though it weighs 50 tonnes the Striker 4500 can speed across the runway at 112 kilometres per hour on its eight wheels.

BIG FACT The boom on the Bronto F174 HDT can rise 53 metres into the air.

Bronto boom

Make it yourself

Make a box model fire engine
with a telescopic ladder.

You will need:

An adult
to help

Paints

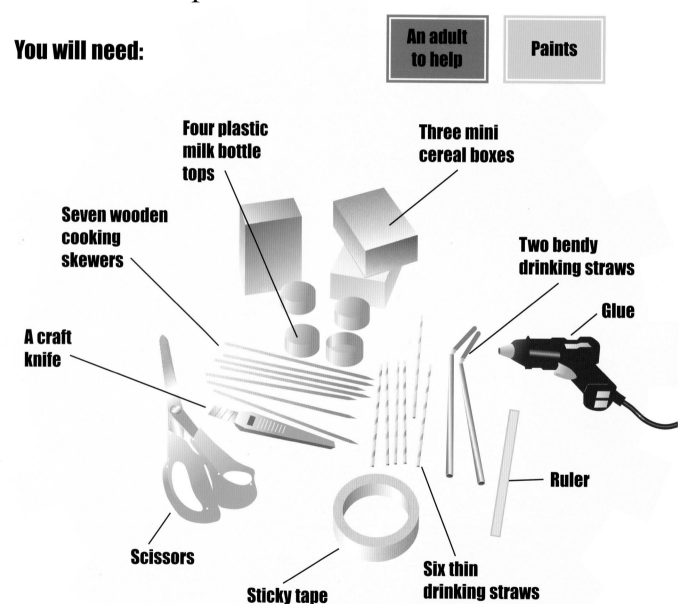

Four plastic
milk bottle
tops

Three mini
cereal boxes

Seven wooden
cooking
skewers

Two bendy
drinking straws

Glue

A craft
knife

Scissors

Ruler

Sticky tape

Six thin
drinking straws

SAFETY! An adult must help you with the cutting and sticking.

1. Cut fourteen 5cm lengths of plastic straw and two 10cm lengths.

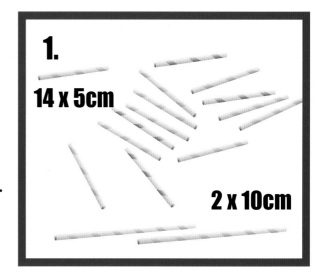

1.

14 x 5cm

2 x 10cm

2. Push a wooden skewer through one end of a short length of straw, as shown. The straw is a rung on the ladder.

2.

3.

3. Add six more rungs. Complete the ladder with a second skewer at the other side of the rungs.

Make a second ladder in the same way.

4. Bend down the ends of a 10cm length of straw to make it the same width as your ladder. Push the pointed ends of the skewers into the bends as shown. You can use the bent lengths of straw to join ladders together.

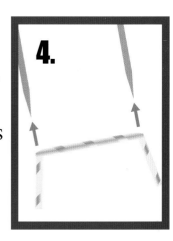

4.

5. Glue/tape the three boxes together to make the fire engine body.

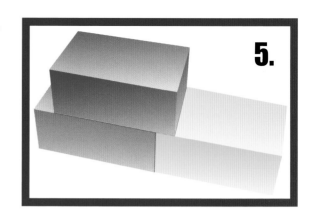

5.

6. Cut a slot at the back of the body for the ladder.

Push a skewer through the body and the straws at the bottom of one of the ladders. Make sure the hole is quite tight. Cut the skewer to length.

Use skewers and bottle tops to give your fire engine wheels as shown.

6.

8.

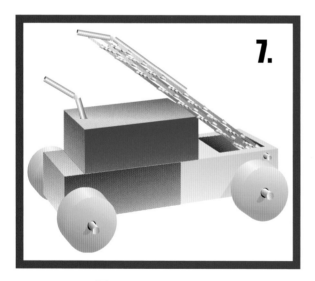

7.

7. Use bendy straws to add monitors (water cannons) to the top ladder section and the fire engine cab.

8. Raise the ladder on your engine!

Trace your own fire engine

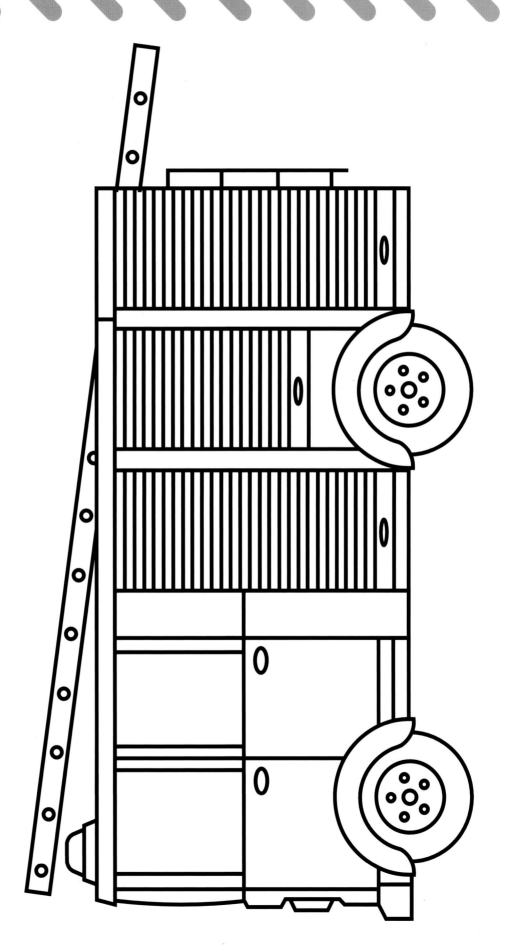

Fire engine words

cab
The part of the fire engine in which a driver sits.

chemical protection suit
A special all-over suit worn by a firefighter to protect him or her from dangerous chemicals.

diesel
The fuel a fire engine uses to make it go.

firefighter
A member of a fire crew whose job is to fight fires.

fire hydrant
A pipe and tap joined to the water pipe under a road. A fire engine can get water from a hydrant to fight a fire.

hose
A flexible (bendy) tube for carrying water.

hydraulic boom
A mechanical arm that unfolds to reach high places. The force to raise the boom comes from hydraulic rams.

monitor
A powerful water cannon.

nozzle
The metal part on the end of a hose, used to direct the water.

pump
A machine for making water or oil move through a pipe or hose.

satellite navigation
A computer map on a screen that shows where a fire engine is, and the best route to an emergency.

siren
A machine that makes a very loud wailing sound.

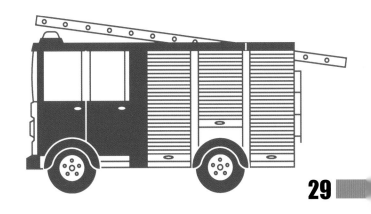

Index